THIS BOOK BELONGS TO

- -

- -

For Madeleine and Theo – RLO

For Eliza – LB

For Chloe – David O'Connell

EGMONT

We bring stories to life

Cover and interior illustrations by David O'Connell
Special thanks to Rebecca Lewis-Oakes and Liz Bankes

Text first published in Great Britain in 2020
by Egmont Books UK Ltd
2 Minster Court, London EC3R 7BB

Text copyright © 2020 Egmont Books UK Ltd
Illustrations copyright © 2020 David O'Connell

ISBN 978 1 4052 9716 5

www.egmontbooks.co.uk

70885/006

A CIP catalogue record for this title is available from the British Library

Printed and bound in Great Britain by CPI Group

THE NAUGHTIEST UNICORN

ON A SCHOOL TRIP

PIP BIRD

ILLUSTRATED BY DAVID O'CONNELL

EGMONT

Contents

CHAPTER ONE
Tick Tock, Tick Tock

Tick tock, tick tock, BRRRRRRRRRRRRRR!

'Good morning, Rani!' said Mira as her big sister opened her eyes.

'GGAAAARRRRRGH!!!' Rani screamed. 'Why are you in my face?!'

Mira threw down the alarm clock and started jumping up and down on her sister's bed. 'We've got to get to Unicorn School! It's MY SCHOOL TRIP TODAY!' Mira yelled. She was waving her signed permission slip in the air. 'I'm almost ready! I just need to make my packed lunch.'

1

'Get OFF!' Rani shoved Mira off the bed and stuck her head under the pillow.

Mira jumped on to the floor, hopping from foot to foot. 'What do you think I should have in my sandwiches, tuna or cheese?'

'GO AWAY!' Rani flung a pillow at her little sister.

'Okay, bye! See you downstairs!' Mira dodged the pillow and scooped up their cat Pickles for a cuddle on the way.

Soon, she'd be cuddling Dave, her UBFF (unicorn best friend forever). He was the best unicorn in the world. Sure, he could be pretty grumpy. And he ALWAYS wanted to eat snacks or have a nap and this often got them both into trouble. And he certainly wasn't as glittery as some of the other unicorns (he was much more farty). BUT Dave was Mira's UBFF and they always ended up having the most brilliant adventures and LOADS of fun.

Unicorn School was Mira's favourite place in the whole world. They went on quests around the Fearsome Forest, hung out with Darcy and Raheem and their unicorns AND earned medals. She couldn't wait to go back!

ᴗᴗᴗ

After Mira had made her sandwiches (she'd decided on cheese) and had some breakfast, it was time to get dressed.

'I wish I could wear my kitticorn pyjamas to

school, Pickles,' Mira said, stroking the picture of the adorable kitticorn on her PJs. A kitticorn was a super cute baby cat that had a horn just like a unicorn. She'd found a book about them in the Unicorn School library and ever since then she'd been OBSESSED – drawing tons of pictures of them, keeping a list of her Top Ten Kitticorn Facts and making her very own kitticorn toy out of cotton wool and a loo roll (even though Rani said it looked more like a weird pig).

Mira was longing to meet

a kitticorn in real life, but they were VERY rare. She was planning to ask the Unicorn School teachers if they'd ever seen one. But first she had to get to Unicorn School!

As soon as Mira and Rani were dressed, it was time to leave. Rani was still grumbling about having to get up so early, but Mira was so excited about her very first Unicorn School trip that she chatted non-stop in the car on the way to the Magic Portal, and all the way round the supermarket.

Most people brought their unicorns treats like hay or carrots. But Dave liked doughnuts best of all. Unfortunately the shop didn't have any doughnuts, so Mira brought some custard cream biscuits instead. She'd read that custard creams were a kitticorn's favourite food, and so she was sure Dave would like them, too! They were on offer so she got five packets.

Mira checked and double-checked her bag for her packed lunch and permission slip. She didn't want anything to get in the way of her first school trip. She didn't even know where they were going yet! It was all so exciting.

When they arrived at the Magic Portal, it wasn't as busy as usual. It was only Mira's class, Class Red, who had a school trip and had to arrive super early. There was something extra special about being at the portal before most other people had got there, and before the sun was even properly up. It felt like going on holiday!

'Have a lovely school trip, Mira!' said Mum, giving her a big hug, while Rani yawned loudly in her ear.

'Thanks, Mum. Oh look, there's Raheem!' Mira ran towards Raheem, waving back at her mum. 'See you soooooooon!'

Raheem was one of Mira's best friends at Unicorn School. Along with Darcy, the three of them always had brilliant adventures. Raheem was clutching his briefcase and looking a bit bleary-eyed. Mira sprinted over and knocked him off balance with a huge hug.

'Woohoo! Are you ready for this?!' she yelled in his ear.

'Um, yes, hello!' Raheem mumbled through
a yawn.

'Then LET'S GO!' Mira dragged Raheem
over to the portal, which was in some bushes
behind the bins. On the way she listed her top
five favourite kitticorn colours to wake him
up a bit. When they reached the bushes,

Mira reached out for the sparkles and –

FFFFZzzzzz   **WHUMPFFFFF**

Twinkly lights exploded around them as they
zoomed upwards, as if they were being sucked
up a helter-skelter by a rainbow vacuum cleaner.
As quickly as they whooshed upwards, they were
suddenly hurtling back down again. Soft pink
and gold rays of the rising sun shone in their eyes
as they tumbled on to the landing haystack and
rolled out into the Grand Paddock.

Mira took a deep breath and looked around.
Right away she spotted something new. Next to
the landing haystack was a big rainbow-coloured
BUS!

'Do you think that's for the school trip? I can't wait to find out where we're going!' Mira squealed, squeezing Raheem in excitement.

Just then, they heard a –

'TA-DAAA!' It was Darcy, spinning over to them with a wheelie. She gave Mira and Raheem a high five. 'Hi team. Missed you! Shall we find our –'

Before Darcy had a chance to finish, two unicorns came cantering over. Star and Brave were Darcy and Raheem's unicorns, and today they were wearing the presents that Darcy and Raheem had made them on an earlier visit to Unicorn School. Brave was wearing Raheem's special homemade superhero cape, while Star was in a wig that Darcy had made her so they would have matching hair.

Star and Brave gave their humans a nuzzle. But where was Dave?

Mira looked around for her Unicorn Best Friend Forever. Down the hill, the school turrets and clocktower gleamed in the rising sun. Beyond the school, Mira could see the Fearsome Forest, and beyond that the sparkly Crystal Mountains. It was all so magical, but there was still no sign of Dave.

Miss Glitterhorn, the Class Red teacher, appeared by the side of the bus, drinking from a very big mug of tea and yawning. She put the tea down and clapped her hands.

'Good morning, Class Red!' she called.

'Gooooood moooooorrrning, Miss Glitterhorrrrn,' called the children, sounding a bit more tired than usual.

'Hi, Mum!' shouted Flo, who'd fallen asleep and woken up with a start.

'Please line up with your unicorns for the school trip,' said Miss Glitterhorn. 'We are leaving shortly. Have your permission slips ready!'

Mira quickly checked – yes, she still had her permission slip. But where was her unicorn? She didn't want him to miss the school trip!

'Dave? Da-ave!' Mira called quietly, ducking behind the bus to see if she could spot him.

Colin the Caretaker was filling up the bus with

13

rainbow-berry juice. The pump was attached
to a long line of tubes all coming from different
rainbow-berry trees at the edge of the forest.

Colin suddenly looked confused. He took
the pump out of the bus and shook it. It looked
like the juice had dried up.

There was a sudden *slurp* sound behind her.
Mira looked around and saw a plump unicorn
bottom poking out of the rainbow-berry trees.
There was her unicorn!

'Dave!' she whispered.

The little unicorn turned and gave her

a wave with his front hoof. He had one of the pipes in his mouth and was guzzling up the rainbow-berry juice!

'There you are!' Mira said with a giggle and ran over to give him a big hug.

By distracting Dave with a slightly sticky toffee she found in her pocket, Mira managed to get the pipe off him and reconnect it to the pump. Colin started whistling happily as the juice began flowing into the bus again. Dave gave a series of cheerful burps.

'Dave, we have to line up with the others. We're going on a trip today!' Mira tried to wipe off the rainbow-berry stains from around Dave's mouth with the end of her sleeve, but she just ended up covered in the berry juice too. 'That's a bit better. Come on!'

Usually Mira had to drag Dave everywhere because he was either asleep or he would sit down and refuse to move. But right now Dave seemed very over-excited. Mira wondered if it was because of all the super-sweet rainbow-berry juice and the toffee. Instead of just trotting back to the bus, Dave zoomed backwards and forwards across the grass, knocking into trees and still burping loudly. Then he started doing all his best prancing moves. Eventually Mira managed to push the little prancing unicorn around to the bus just as Miss Glitterhorn was ticking the last of her classmates off the register.

'And, good! That's everyone. Oh!' said Miss Glitterhorn. 'Dave – you look . . . rather unusual this morning?'

Mira looked properly at her unicorn. His mane had turned rainbow-coloured. It must have been the rainbow-berry juice!

'Um, Dave just wanted to . . . look nice for the school trip?' Mira said. She hoped her teacher wouldn't ask any more questions.

'How lovely,' said Miss Glitterhorn vaguely.

Phew, thought Mira. Surely soon they would find out where they were going and then the school trip could begin!

CHAPTER TWO
All Aboard the Rainbow Bus!

The Unicorn School head teacher, Madame Shetland, joined Miss Glitterhorn at the bus.

'Welcome back to Unicorn School, Class Red,' yawned Madame Shetland. 'Are you ready for your first school trip?'

They all cheered and Darcy started a Mexican wave.

'Yes, it is jolly exciting,' agreed Madame Shetland sleepily. 'Especially as this school trip will also involve a special quest.'

A ripple of excitement ran through Class Red. Mira wondered if there'd be an opportunity to win a medal!

Madame Shetland shushed the class. 'So, today you will be going to BARCC. Miss Glitterhorn will tell you all you need to know on the way there.'

Raheem nudged Mira. 'We have to . . . bark? Like a dog? I'm a bit scared of dogs.'

'WOOF!' barked Flo.

Mira was almost too excited to speak. 'No, no!' she said, hopping from one foot to the other. 'BARCC stands for Baby Animal Rainbow Care Centre. It's where they look after lots of animals and their babies. And they sometimes have . . .

they sometimes have . . .'

Mira could feel her cheeks flushing and her tummy was fluttering with excitement.

'What?' asked Darcy. 'You look weird.'

'KITTICORNS!' exploded Mira. 'They're like the cutest things EVER!'

'Kitticorns are great,' agreed Flo. 'They're my fourth favourite animals after sloths, llamas and goblins.'

'Meh,' said Darcy. 'I'm a dog person. Kittens stare at you with those creepy eyes that are too big for their faces, you know? Like, what are they thinking?'

Mira frowned at her friend. 'Darcy, they are the cutest things EVER. Did you know, kitticorns can be all colours of the rainbow, but the *official* cutest ones are gold? They're very rare and super special.'

Dave snorted loudly and shook his rainbow mane.

'Oh, you're super-special too, Dave,' said Mira quickly, giving him a comforting pat. 'But kitticorns are THE most special super-cute special things in the ENTIRE WORLD.'

Dave looked cross and farted.

'If you say so, Mira,' said Darcy with a shrug. 'There'd better be a gift shop at this place.'

Miss Glitterhorn clapped her hands. 'Now, have you all got your packed lunches?'

'I HAVE!' Mira shouted, waving her lunchbox

22

in the air. It was newly covered in kitticorn stickers. Inside were the cheese sandwiches she'd made earlier, plus an apple, a satsuma and a box of raisins. Plus, her mum had let her have a packet of crisps AND a chocolate biscuit. And she had all the custard creams for Dave.

'We've *all* got lunchboxes, Mira,' scoffed Jake, rolling his eyes. 'My dad put FOUR chocolate biscuits in mine.'

Mira stuck her tongue out at Jake. He always had to boast about *something*.

The teacher clapped her hands. 'Okay, time to get on the bus! On you g— yes, Darcy?'

Darcy put her hand up. 'Miss, I need a wee,' she said.

'Does anyone else need to use the toilet?' asked Miss Glitterhorn.

Everyone except Flo put their hands up.

'Right, everyone quickly go to the stableyard to use the outdoor loos,' Miss Glitterhorn instructed. 'Please make sure your unicorns have had a chance to go as well.'

Mira lined up with the rest of her class for the toilets, then took Dave over to the unicorn loo to do his business. Unicorn poos were usually small

and glittery, but not Dave's. He did giant sloppy
poos which took Mira quite a long time to clean
up. Mira was worried they might miss the bus,
so she snuck Dave a biscuit from her lunchbox
to hurry him up. She was pleased to see that he
DID like custard creams.

'Dave, you and kitticorns have something in
common – you BOTH love the same biscuits!'
she told him happily.

Dave frowned and spat the custard cream out
on the floor. They both looked at it, and Dave
ate it again. And then he did a giant poo. Mira
sighed. She whipped out the foldable poo shovel
she now always carried in her pocket and got
to work.

Miss Glitterhorn was looking at her watch

and tapping her foot when the class returned to the bus. 'Good, right, children. We really must be going now. Yes, Flo?'

Flo put her hand down. 'I need a wee.'

Miss Glitterhorn sighed loudly. 'Why didn't you go when everyone else did?'

'I was busy plaiting Sparkles' hair,' Flo explained. 'She wanted to look nice for the trip.' Flo's unicorn, Sparkles, flicked her fishtail plait over one shoulder.

'Okay! Fine,' said Miss Glitterhorn. 'Quickly, please, go and use the toilets. Everyone else, please put on a high-visibility vest. We need to be able to spot you around the farm.'

Colin the Caretaker brought out a box of neon

yellow vests. Jake got to it first and spent ages rummaging through the box.

'Jake, hurry up, please,' said Miss Glitterhorn. She was starting to sound exasperated.

'I just want to make sure I get the best one,' said Jake.

'They're all identical, Jake,' said Darcy, wheeling over and grabbing the top one off the pile. 'It's how you wear them that matters.'

Everyone put one on, including the unicorns.

Finally Class Red and their unicorns all filed on to the bus.

Jake was pushing past everyone, trying to get to the back seat. 'Everyone knows that the cool people sit at the back,' he said.

Mira had wanted to get the back seats for her, Raheem and Darcy, but Jake was too quick. He scrambled on board, dragging his unicorn Pegasus with him, and jumped onto the back seat, next to Tamsin and her unicorn, Moondance.

'YES!' yelled Jake. 'Me and Pegasus are the BEST at buses!'

'Get comfortable, everyone,' called Miss

Glitterhorn from the front. 'It's a long journey.'

'Once we were going on holiday and the car journey was eight hours,' said Jake smugly.

'Once I got so carsick I threw up all over my mum's head,' said Tamsin, next to him.

Jake stood up in alarm.

'No switching seats! Sit down please, Jake,' said Miss Glitterhorn.

Mira, Raheem and Darcy all found seats, one behind the other. Mira leaned over to do up Dave's seatbelt and accidentally tickled his tummy. Dave started to do his Dave laugh, which was a loud HAW HAW sound that Raheem found a bit frightening, but Mira thought was one of the best sounds in the world. She tickled his belly again and Dave laughed loudly.

Once the whole class was in their seats, the doors closed. And finally, they set off up the Unicorn School drive, into the Fearsome Forest!

'Woohoo, school trip!' shouted Darcy, flinging her hands in the air.

Seb and his unicorn, Firework, started beatboxing while the class chanted, 'School! Trip! School! Trip!' except Flo, who was yelling, 'Sloths, sloths, sloths!'

Miss Glitterhorn clapped her hands several times to get their attention. 'Please stop cheering, so I can make the safety announcements!' she shouted.

'Yay!' cheered Raheem.

'Firstly, please stay seated on the bus at all times

with your seatbelts on,' Miss Glitterhorn said.

Darcy's hand shot up. 'But, miss, you're standing,' she said.

Miss Glitterhorn sighed. 'I will sit as soon as I have completed the announcements, thank you, Darcy.'

'Maybe you could hook your seatbelt round your leg?' said Darcy, helpfully.

'Thank you, Darcy. Anyway!' said Miss Glitterhorn. 'We are on our way to BARCC. This is a very important school trip to learn all about the animals in our world and how to take care of them –'

Both Jake and Darcy had their hands up.

'What about the quest?' said Jake.

'Yes, there will be a quest,' said Miss Glitterhorn. 'This will be explained in more detail when we're there. Mira, do you have a question?'

Mira had her hand up as far as it would go and was waving it around madly. 'Are there kitticorns at BARCC?' she blurted out.

An *oooooooh* rippled around the bus.

Miss Glitterhorn smiled. 'Well, I believe that there currently *are* caticorns at BARCC, which means there might also be kitticorns! So, if we're very lucky, we just might see them. BUT they are very shy animals, so don't get your hopes up.'

Mira squealed and leaned forward to talk

to Darcy. 'Even Rani didn't see any kitticorns when she went to BARCC. I can't believe we might get to see some of the most awesome, cute creatures in the whole world!'

'They can't possibly be cuter than us, Star,' said Darcy, and she took a quick selfie with her unicorn on her phone.

The road was getting a bit bumpy and Miss Glitterhorn gripped the seats in front of her to stay on her feet.

'Oops!' she said. 'Where was I? So, what's really important about this trip to BARCC is that we learn how to care for our animal friends and the world around us. So, pay attention at the centre and – whooooaaaa!'

The bus turned a sharp corner and Miss
Glitterhorn tumbled on to the front seat.

Everyone giggled but Mira stared out of
the window, lost in a daydream where she was
cuddling lots of gorgeous, furry kitticorns . . .

CHAPTER THREE
Are We Nearly There Yet?

Class Red had been on the bus for an hour already and were nearly at the top of the Crystal Mountains. Mira turned round to look through the back window of the bus. Behind them lay the Fearsome Forest. They'd never been this far away from Unicorn School before!

For the last twenty minutes they had been playing lots of fun games, including Burp Alphabet (which Miss Glitterhorn had quickly banned). Now they were playing a game called

Would You Rather, which Mira's sister had taught her.

'Would you rather have a bum for a face or a face for a bum?' said Darcy. Most people went for a bum face.

'Would you rather have a pet sloth or a pet kitticorn?' said Mira. Everyone except Flo said that one was really hard.

'Would you rather eat a poo or wear a hat made of poo forever?' said Darcy. Most people chose a poo hat.

'Would you rather have a pet kitticorn or a UBFF?' said Freya, and all the unicorns snorted crossly. Everyone said UBFF, except Mira who said 'Fluff' because she was daydreaming about what she would call her pet kitticorn.

'Would you rather eat a poo or have *Dave* as your UBFF?' said Jake, with a mean grin.

Everyone gasped and looked at Mira and Dave.

'Actually maybe Scamp . . . what?' said Mira, still in her daydream.

'I would rather eat a poo than sit next to *Jake*!' said Darcy, defending Mira and Dave.

'Well I would rather LIVE in a poo than sit next to you!' Jake called back.

'Well I would rather be MADE OF poo than have to sit next to YOU!' shouted Darcy.

Then Miss Glitterhorn said that all games mentioning poo were banned and why didn't they play something nice like I Spy.

'I spy something beginning with P,' said Darcy.

Miss Glitterhorn gave her a warning look.

Soon it was Mira's turn.

'I spy . . .' said Mira, 'something beginning with . . . S.'

'Sloths?' guessed Flo.

'No.'

'Spiders?' Freya called out. Brave, Raheem's unicorn, whimpered. He was just a teensy little bit scared of spiders.

'Nope!' said Mira.

Freya tried again. 'Snow-capped mountain?'

Raheem tutted. 'That doesn't count as an "s", because "mountain" begins with a –'

'Yes, that's right!' said Mira quickly. 'Your turn!'

The bus started going down the other side of the Crystal Mountains. The road was steep and very twisty.

Freya thought for a minute. 'I spy . . . something beginning with . . .'

'Sssssss,' said Tamsin.

'It's MY turn!' said Freya with a frown.

'Can't we have another letter?' said Raheem.

'Ssssick!' Tamsin was groaning and looked rather green. She was clutching her tummy. 'I feel sick. Miss! I feel sick.'

Miss Glitterhorn

quickly ushered Tamsin to the front and gave her a bag to be sick in. 'Will someone please swap seats with Tamsin?' she asked.

Dave was already moving back to sit in Tamsin's seat. Mira quickly followed him.

Jake grumbled as he moved to let them sit down. 'Make sure your unicorn doesn't fart near Pegasus,' he said. 'It upsets him.'

Mira gave Dave a protective pat, and Dave let out a gigantic fart. Pegasus turned to face the window. Then Flo popped her head over the seat in front, quickly followed by her unicorn, Sparkles. Flo started asking Mira a million questions about the kitticorns.

'What do they eat? Where do they sleep?

Which eats more, a kitticorn or a puppicorn?

What do they like to play with?'

Mira took a deep breath and answered.

'Kitticorn treats, somewhere warm and smelly,

a puppicorn and balls of rainbow wool.

Kitticorns can bounce the balls on their noses!'

Flo squeaked. 'Sooo adorable!'

'Yup,' agreed Mira with an enormous grin. 'I have a book called *Kitticornucopia*. I can't believe we are going to get to snuggle and cuddle them and kiss their little kitticorny faces!'

Something suddenly hit the side of Mira's head. It was her apple. She turned to see Dave had opened her lunchbox. Dave picked up the apple again and threw it in the air, trying to bounce it on his nose. This time it flew across the back seats and landed on Pegasus's horn. Mira leaned over, pulled the apple free and put it back in her lunchbox.

'Psst,' Raheem whispered to get Mira's attention. 'What do you think the quest is? Miss Glitterhorn didn't really say anything.

Do you think it's a test?'

'I don't know. I'm sure it will be fine, Raheem,' said Mira.

Darcy waved her hand in the air. 'Miss, are we nearly there yet?'

Miss Glitterhorn sighed. 'No, Darcy. We're about halfway. Look, here's the map of BARCC to be looking at in the meantime.'

Mira spotted BARCC first. Sunlight was glinting off the gold-rimmed rainbow sign on the gates.

'We're here! We're here!' she cried.

The rest of Class Red stood up to see, and Miss Glitterhorn had to ask them to sit down again. Colin the Caretaker tooted the Rainbow Bus horn as they passed through the farm gates and everybody cheered. As soon as the bus stopped, all the pupils and unicorns scrambled off the bus.

'Come back, class!' Miss Glitterhorn was trying to get everyone to line up back at the bus. 'Mira, stop jumping up and down.'

'WHERE ARE THE KITTICORNS?!' Mira yelled.

'And also calm down, please,' said the teacher.

'Well, hello there kids, you must be Class Red

from Unicorn School!' said a voice.

'What is THAT?' Darcy looked appalled as she wheeled off the ramp.

A muddy green tractor, pulling a large trailer, tooted its horn and pulled to a stop next to the Rainbow Bus. Out jumped a short, wide man with large socks rolled over his hiking boots, long straggly hair and a wiry grey beard. He had his hands on his hips and lots of things sticking out of pockets all over his shirt and shorts.

'Good morning, everyone! I'm Bruce Hasslehoof, chief warden here at the Baby Animal Rainbow Care Centre. Let's get ready to rumble!'

Raheem shivered and nudged Mira. 'I don't want to rumble.'

Mira tried to give him a reassuring pat on the shoulder, but she couldn't stop grinning at the thought of kitticorns being somewhere nearby!

'We have a super-exciting day planned for you all. We're going to take a tour round the farm in this tractor trailer, stop off for the morning's awesome activity, then have lunch, then enjoy this afternoon's awesome activity,' Bruce explained.

Darcy's hand shot up. 'What are the awesome activities?'

'It's a surprise!' said Bruce, winking at Darcy.

'Is it really true that there are kitticorns here?' Mira asked. She had stopped jumping but was now hopping from foot to foot.

Bruce smiled. 'Yes! There is a caticorn here with her kitticorns. But they're tucked away somewhere, safe in their nest. Caticorns are easily scared, you know!' He clapped his hands. 'Come on into the yard, kids, and get some wellies on you and your unicorns. There's a lot of mud around!'

Bruce and Miss Glitterhorn started ushering the children past the tractor and over to the welly station.

Dave sniffed loudly and started trotting in the opposite direction, towards the Visitor Centre and café. Mira gave him some crisps to tempt him back to the wellies. After wrestling with his hooves for quite some time, she decided that three out of four wellies wasn't too bad and gave up on the last one.

Everyone else had already gathered by the

tractor trailers, where Bruce was splitting Class

Red into groups of four and handing out clipboards. Raheem hugged his clipboard to his chest like it was a comfort blanket.

Bruce ushered the children and unicorns into the tractor trailers. Mira was in a group with Darcy, Raheem and Jake. Darcy and Jake pulled faces at each other.

'Right!' called Bruce with a great big smile. 'So, you can use your clipboard to jot down stuff you see and draw pictures – whatever you like. Awesome activity number one, here we come!'

'What about the health and safety briefing?' asked Raheem.

'Oh! Yes,' said Bruce. 'Well, the first rule at

BARCC is to stay where I can see you at all times.'

Raheem happily wrote down the rule down on his clipboard.

Bruce carried on. 'And the second rule at BARCC is do NOT take the baby animals home. No matter how cute they are, BARCC is the best place for them!'

'What about the quest?' asked Jake. 'Can I be leader?'

Bruce laughed. 'You're a keen bean, I like you,' he said. Mira rolled her eyes at Darcy. 'Well, there is a quest, but we don't need a leader. And anyway, no one has completed it since I did, back when I was at Unicorn School!'

Darcy gasped. 'What, not in a million years?'

Bruce frowned. 'I'm not quite that old, young lady.' He dug out a stack of cards from one of his many pockets and started handing them out. 'You can attach this to your clipboards. Don't worry if you don't have time to complete it. You'll probably be having too much fun learning all about the baby animals here at BARCC!'

BARCC QUEST.
CAN YOU SPOT . . .

What is brown and sometimes sticky but is not a stick?

....

What has ears but cannot hear?

....

What has a bark but no bite?

....

What hisses but is not a snake?

....

An amazing sight inside which you cannot see?

....

'Ooh! I love riddles,' said Mira.

'This makes literally no sense,' said Darcy.

'I thought nothing was going to bark at me,' muttered Raheem.

'And, finally, the third rule at BARCC is no eating anything anywhere except the picnic meadow,' said Bruce. 'The baby animals here are on very specific diets, and we don't want to make them poorly.'

There was a loud neigh from Dave that sounded a bit like 'NOOOOOOOOOOOOO!'

'Good luck, children,' said Miss Glitterhorn. 'Now, since you'll be doing self-directed work on this trip, I'll just stay behind in the café and look after the shoes. Have fun!'

CHAPTER FOUR
Tap Tap Tap – Crack!

Mira was trying to get comfortable in the tractor trailer when she felt something tugging at her backpack. She looked around and saw Dave was nibbling on her bag strap. She quietly snuck him a biscuit, hoping Bruce wouldn't notice. Even though the third rule at BARCC was no eating except in the picnic meadow, she thought one tiny custard cream couldn't hurt. And Dave NEVER left behind any crumbs.

The tractor started up with a loud rev and Bruce rubbed his hands together. 'Right-o, kids!

This is the exciting bit. You can see on your right there is the sparklecorn field, which is at the centre of the farm. As you know, this crop is turned into hay for unicorns and other animals, but it has many other amazing uses. As well as unicorn feed, it is used for unicorn bedding, arts and crafts materials and even unicorn toilets!'

Raheem was taking notes on everything Bruce said. Nobody else was, although Flo had drawn a picture of a sloth climbing up the sparklecorn.

'Goats! Look! Left!' shouted Flo.

Everyone scooted over to the left-hand side of the trailer, making it lean dangerously on two wheels. They waved to the goats and baby goats in small fields.

Darcy giggled. 'That goat is eating a welly.' She pointed to a BARCC warden who was hopping on one foot, chasing a baby goat around a field. The baby did indeed have a welly in its mouth.

'It's a goaticorn,' said Raheem, making a note of it on his clipboard. 'And, yes, a goaticorn will eat anything if it's hungry enough.'

'Just like you, Dave!' said Darcy.

Mira was about to defend her unicorn when she was distracted by Dave trying to get another biscuit by opening the zip of her rucksack with his teeth.

'Now we are passing the sheepicorn station,' Bruce continued. 'You can see the wardens feeding the baby lambicorns with extra milk from a bottle.'

'Toooooo cuuuuuute!' Flo gasped.

Bruce pointed out the cowicorns and pigicorns in the farm zone. They also passed a sign for the Cuddle Corner.

'What's that?' asked Flo.

'Oh, that's just the llamacorns, slothicorns and koalacorns,' said Bruce. 'Not as awesome as our first awesome activity.'

There was only one thing cuter than koalacorns, Mira thought. MAYBE they were going to find and play with the kitticorns as their first activity! That really *would* be awesome.

'Here we are!' announced Bruce.

The tractors pulled up at two red barns and the children excitedly helped their unicorns out of the trailers. There were flecks of rainbow straw lying around the door of one barn. Raheem immediately started sketching the barn on the piece of paper on his clipboard.

Bruce strode to the front of the group, unlatched the door and pulled back the barn door to reveal . . .

'It's just full of dirt,' said Mira. 'Where are the animals?'

Bruce laughed. 'There are LOT of tiny animals in here, but they're just too small to see.

This is the Soil Barn! Awesome activity number one is . . . soil sieving! We're going to look very carefully at what the soil is made of and how it supports life on the farm.'

'Are you joking?' asked Darcy.

Cheep cheep!

'What was that?' asked Mira.

'Oh that's just the chickicorn hatching barn next door,' said Bruce. 'Now, my favourite thing about soil –'

Bruce didn't have time to finish as Class Red stampeded over to the chickicorn barn. He only just made it to the doors before them.

'STOP! Stay with the soil!' he screeched.

Rainbow-coloured straw fluttered out into

the farmyard with a chorus of *cheep-cheep*ing.
Class Red surged forward again.

'Well, I suppose we can have a quick look
before we start soil sieving,' said Bruce with a
sigh. 'So *this* is the chickicorn hatching barn.'

There were bales of rainbow straw piled up
on each side of the barn, and different-coloured
henicorns sitting on eggs in nests. At the far end
there were two long tables with rows of lights
dangling above them. Under each light was a
carefully made rainbow nest with one or two
eggs inside.

'Chickicorns hatch when their eggs are warm
and cosy. Now, some of our henicorns lay so
many eggs they can't sit on them all. That's

why we have these hot lights over some nests. It's called incubating,' explained Bruce. 'And it's very important that no one disturbs the incubating process. Otherwise the chickicorns could hatch and become confused. So don't touch anything!'

Class Red gathered round the hatching tables.

'Is anything actually going to happen?' asked Darcy.

'Shh,' said Bruce. 'Yes, if we're quiet, we just might hear an egg cracking.'

The children waited.

The eggs stayed very still.

'I don't hear anything,' said Darcy again.

'SHH!' said Bruce again. 'The conditions for hatching need to be just right.'

As all the Class Red pupils stood quietly,
Mira heard Dave's tummy rumble. Then, before
she could stop him, he quickly licked one of the
multi-coloured eggs!

'Dave, no!' Mira hissed. 'It's an egg, not a sweet!'

Tap tap tap.

'What's THAT?' asked Darcy.

'That's a hatching sound, SHHHH EVERYONE!'

Mira thought Bruce's shushing was louder than Darcy's talking, but then there was another

. . .

Tap tap tap – crack!

A small hole appeared in the top of the egg in front of Dave.

Tap tap crack crack tap crack TAP CRACK.

A tiny, bent horn emerged from the eggshell, followed by a pale blue fluffy chickicorn. It gave an adorable *cheep* and shook the rest of the shell off its back. It stared at Dave.

Dave stared at it. Then the chickicorn jumped on to Dave's nose and nestled in his mane.

Cheep! it cheeped.

'Awww,' said Flo. 'It thinks your hair is rainbow straw!'

Dave shook his head. The chickicorn rolled back down his nose and into the nesting box. It sat up, hopped up Dave's nose and snuggled into his mane again. Dave kept shaking his head, but the chickicorn was clinging on tightly now with its beak.

CHEEP! it cheeped happily.

Dave seemed to have started a trend. There was more tapping and cracking, and lots of

65

colourful little fluffy chickicorns were hatching all over the table and jumping all over the place.

'I've never seen so many hatch at once!' cried Bruce in a panic. 'Quick, we've got to get the babies back into their nests!'

Class Red didn't need telling twice. They all started running around, trying to catch the baby chickicorns and scoop them back into their nests.

By the time they'd rounded up all the chickicorns, the morning was almost over.

'No time for soil sieving,' said Bruce, shaking his head sadly.

'Oh no,' said Darcy.

'You're right – it's a real shame,' said Bruce, brightening up. 'Maybe I can swap the afternoon activity –'

'NO!' shouted Class Red.

Everyone saw Bruce's face fall.

'We mean, you just explained it so well,' said
Mira quickly. 'We've all noted down lots of facts
and drawn the soil.'

The class nodded.

'I actually have done that,' said Raheem.

'That's great!' said Bruce, looking pleased. 'I
guess it's time for lunch then.'

At the word 'lunch', there was a loud SMASH
as Dave bolted through the barn doors and raced
towards the trailer.

CHAPTER FIVE
Picnic Time

Everyone was very pleased to get to the picnic field (and to get out of the soil sieving). They were having their lunch in a wildflower meadow, where red and white checked picnic blankets had been laid out. Next to the field there was a little pond with a bridge over it, with a family of duckicorns swimming about. In the field to the right was a bullicorn and its baby. Even though the animals were grazing peacefully, they were still a bit on the scary side with their red eyes and sharp horns.

Class Red lined up to collect a bag of hay for their unicorns. Then they all sat down on the picnic blankets and opened up their lunchboxes.

Jake was sitting behind Mira, Raheem and Darcy with his unicorn, Pegasus.

'Hey!' shouted Jake. 'Dave's eaten three of my four chocolate biscuits!'

Mira turned around and looked in Jake's lunchbox. There were indeed three empty chocolate biscuit wrappers. She looked at Dave, who was licking his lips. There was a large smear of chocolate on his nose.

'Well,' said Mira. 'You can't prove it was Dave.'

'I actually saw him eat them,' said Jake.

'I'll swap you a biscuit for your crisps,' said Seb.

'Great teamwork, guys!' said Bruce, clapping
his hands.

'I'll swap you a sandwich for my biscuit,' added
Darcy.

Jake smiled. 'Fine, here you go,' he said, handing
her a square of sandwich.

Darcy shook her head. 'No, the whole thing.'

'But that's not fair!' protested Jake.

Darcy shrugged. 'Come back to me when you have a serious offer.'

Mira gave Dave a whole packet of custard creams to stop him from stealing any more lunches. Then she noticed that Raheem and Brave weren't eating their lunch and were staring intently at the clipboard.

'Are you okay?' asked Mira.

'We're just looking at the quest list to see if we can solve some of the riddles,' said Raheem. 'I'm sure we'll have spotted some things already.'

'I'm not that fussed about the quest,' said Mira, sharing her sandwich with Dave. 'Even though I *would* like to get a medal. But mostly I just want to see a kitticorn.'

Flo sighed into her packet of crisps. 'Me too.'

'Did you know, kitticorn horns are soft and furry when they're first born?' Mira said.

'Nooooooo!'

'Yes!' said Mira happily. 'And if they're feeling playful, they tickle your face with their tail.'

Mira took a sip of her juice, and tried to remember her next favourite kitticorn fact.

She turned back to Flo, but for some reason, Dave's bum was in her face. He swooshed his tail around.

'Bluerghle argle flargh!' As Mira tried to stop Dave's tail tickling her, she spilled her juice. Dave quickly licked it up, then burped grumpily.

'Is Dave okay?' asked Flo.

'Are we playing Burp Alphabet again?' said Seb.

'I think Dave's just hungry,' said Mira, giving her unicorn a bit more sandwich. 'Did you know that if kitticorns want your attention, they wind around your ankles over and over again?'

There was a THUD as Dave dived over the picnic blanket and collided with Mira's ankles, knocking her over.

'Dave!' Mira said. 'Calm down!' She handed him a biscuit. 'And,' Mira went on, turning back to Flo, 'if they REALLY love you, kitticorns roll over and show you their tummies for tickling.'

'Awww!' said Flo.

Dave dropped to the ground, rolled over on to his back and kicked his legs in the air.

Unfortunately, as his legs flailed around, he kicked Sparkles in the nose. Sparkles snorted, stepped back, tripped over Jake's lunchbox and fell into his lap, squashing his last biscuit.

'Arghh, you're all SO annoying!' shouted Jake, pushing Sparkles away.

'Do you think Dave is trying to tell you something?' asked Flo thoughtfully.

'No,' said Mira. 'He's just being Dave.'

Dave plopped himself down on the picnic blanket. For a moment Mira thought he looked sad. Was Flo right?

'MEEARRGH!' whinnied Dave suddenly, and shook his head. 'MEEEEEEEARGH!'

Mira stared at him. It was the strangest sound she'd ever heard.

'Maybe he's trying to tell you that he's got a chickicorn in his mane,' said Flo, nibbling on a crisp.

'WHAT?!'

Mira rushed over to Dave and checked.

Sure enough, there was the baby blue
chickicorn snoozing in Dave's mane. It looked
very cosy.

'Dave, how did this happen?' Mira said.

Dave shrugged. The chickicorn woke up and
*cheep*ed.

'The second rule of BARCC is not to take any

of the baby animals,' said Raheem, worriedly.

Mira gulped. They hadn't *meant* to take the chickicorn, but what if they got into trouble for breaking the rules? What if they didn't get a chance to see a kitticorn?

'We've got to get it back to its barn without Bruce seeing,' Mira said.

'Everything all right over there?' Bruce called over as he packed up the picnic blankets.

The chickicorn *cheep-cheep*ed again and they all shushed it.

'Absolutely fine!' shouted Darcy. 'We were just saying how much we love the soil in this wildflower meadow!'

Bruce beamed. 'Quite right too. Okay kids,

let's get back to the trailers and get on to your second awesome activity for the day!'

'What can be more awesome than sieving soil?' asked Darcy.

'Just you wait and see!' said Bruce with a huge grin, starting up the tractor.

ᑌᑌᑌ

A few minutes later Bruce stopped the tractor.

'Right-o, kids!' he said. 'Here we are in the sparklecorn field. Your second awesome activity today is . . . measuring the sparklecorn!'

All the children and their unicorns slowly climbed down from the trailers. Bruce handed out measuring tapes and charts.

78

Raheem carefully attached the chart to his clipboard and sharpened his pencil.

'We need to measure the sparklecorn each spring to make sure it's healthy and happy. You will see on your measuring tapes the perfect height for each corn stalk,' said Bruce.

Mira unfurled her tape and saw centimetre markings with numbers and pictures. At '1m' there was a picture of a sparklecorn stalk, surrounded by lots of sparkles and words that read, 'Perfect sparklecorn height!'

'Each team of four will have one square metre to measure,' said Bruce. 'I've marked out the areas with rainbow tape. Please measure all the sparklecorn stalks in your patch and write them down on the chart. You have one hour to complete this activity. After that, it'll be almost time for you to go back to Unicorn School. So make the most of it! I'll just be over in the tractor if you need me.'

Jake flung his arms in the air. 'This is going to take for ever!' he moaned. 'What about the quest?'

The chickicorn cheeped loudly from inside Dave's mane and Dave frowned.

Raheem looked up from the clipboard. 'Actually, I think we're doing pretty well on the quest. I've been working out the riddles.'

'Really?' said Mira.

Raheem pointed to the checklist. 'Number one was "what is brown and sticky but is not a stick"?' Well, that's awesome activity one: soil.'

'*Don't* call it awesome,' muttered Darcy.

'And then, "What has ears but cannot hear?",'
continued Raheem. He pointed at the sparklecorn.
'Ears of corn can't hear. I haven't worked out
number three yet – "What has a bark but no bite".'

'The farm monster?' said Darcy.

'That's stupid!' said Jake, but Mira saw him
glancing around.

'Wait, what was number four?' said Mira.

'"What hisses but is not a snake",' said Raheem.

'I KNOW THAT ONE!' shrieked Mira.
'Hissing is just one of the many adorable noises
that a kitticorn makes! That must be the answer!'
An idea suddenly came to her. 'Bruce said we
don't have much time left. Why don't we return
the chickicorn and find the kitticorns at the same

time? AND we might find the missing answers
and complete the quest!'

Jake grinned and punched the air. 'Woo! If we
complete the quest, we win the MEDAL!'
Jake loved medals almost as much as Mira.

'I'm in,' said Darcy. 'This is *actually* awesome.'

Raheem pointed to the measuring tape. 'But what about the activity? We have to measure ALL the corn.'

'Leave that to me,' said Darcy.

She took four sweets out of her lunchbox and held them under Dave's nose. Just as he was about to chomp them, Darcy threw one to each corner of their sparklecorn patch. Dave sped away, the little chickicorn on his head cheeping excitedly – and gobbled up all four biscuits, flattening the entire patch of corn into a neat little square.

Raheem gasped.

'Our corn all comes in at zero centimetres,' said Darcy, writing a big '0' on the clipboard with a flourish. 'So, which way to the chicks?'

'And the kitticorns!' said Mira.

'And the quest!' said Jake.

'Show me the map,' said Darcy. 'Let's do this, Team Awesome!'

CHAPTER SIX
Quests, Chicks and Kitticorns

'We know where the chickicorn barn is, so let's
find the kitticorns first,' said Jake. 'Does anyone
know where they might be?'

'I have LOTS of ideas,' said Mira
enthusiastically.

'Shall we start with one idea, maybe?' Raheem
said, looking at his watch. 'We have to find the
kitticorns AND return the chickicorn AND
complete the quest AND get back before the

school bus leaves . . .'

Mira thought for a minute. 'Well, kitticorns really like to play with glitter daisies. There were lots near the Cuddle Corner. Which way was that?'

Raheem looked at the map on his clipboard. 'We probably shouldn't go round the tractor trail as we don't want Bruce to see us, so we might have to go straight through the sparklecorn field.'

Jake took the map off Raheem and said it was definitely left. Darcy took it off Jake and said it was definitely right. Raheem reached over and carefully turned the map the right way up. Then he pointed to the unicorns, who had all shuffled to face the same way. (Except Dave, who was having a nap. The chickicorn on his head had fallen asleep too and was doing cute little cheepy snores.)

'The unicorns are pointing north,' said Raheem. 'So according to the map, the Cuddle Corner is . . . that way!'

Mira woke up Dave and everyone got on
to their unicorns and headed through the
sparklecorn, one behind the other. The leaves
tickled Dave's ears as they brushed past the stalks
and he gave a series of giggly snorts as he wove
in and out of the tall plants. The chickicorn kept
sneezing.

After a few minutes they reached the Cuddle
Corner. They looked all the way round the fence
twice. There were so many glitter daisies that
the unicorns got sparkles all over their hooves,
but they didn't see any kitticorns. Dave started
snacking on the flowers and got a glittery tongue.

Jake folded his arms. 'You said they'd be here,'
he said to Mira.

'I didn't!' Mira protested. 'I said they *might* be here. Ooh, I know! Kitticorns love to snuggle up in soft wool. Maybe they'll be –'

'Near the baby lambicorns!' cried Darcy. 'This way!'

Raheem pointed in the opposite direction. 'It's actually over there.'

'Yes, that's what I meant,' said Darcy. 'Follow me!' She and Star whirled round and started trotting back through the sparklecorn.

When they reached the baby lambicorns, there was plenty of wool but no kitticorns.

Jake looked very grumpy. 'We're *never* going to find them and finish this quest,' he said. 'Let's just return the silly chickicorn and go back to the stupid sparklecorn measuring activity.'

Cheep, said the chickicorn happily.

Raheem tapped his watch. 'That might be a good idea,' he said.

'No!' cried Mira. 'Let's try one more place. Umm . . . Where else could they be?'

As Mira thought hard, she was distracted by a strange snuffling sound. Turning around she realised that Dave had climbed into a large rubbish bin and was tucking into some old chips.

'Dave!' she shouted crossly. Dave reversed out of the bin. He was eating a chip and there was a banana skin on his horn. The chick was also eating a chip.

Mira suddenly had a brilliant idea.

'The bins!' she yelled.

'What?' asked Jake.

'My book said that kitticorns like to make their
nests in a nice warm place that's a bit smelly. It
puts other animals off finding their nest. There
were some compost bins behind the pigicorn
pens,' Mira said excitedly. 'Let's have one more try,
and if they're not there, then we'll just return the

chickicorn and go back to the bus. Pleeeeease?'

'It'll have to be a very quick look,' said Raheem, looking a bit anxious.

Mira jumped back on to Dave. 'Come on, team – to the pigicorn pens!'

And they charged off through the sparklecorn as quickly as Dave's little legs could carry him, the chickicorn in his mane happily *cheep-cheep*ing away.

The pigicorn pens were easy to find, as they were in front of a very tall tree.
There was a sign on the tree saying it was a 'Doglark' tree and the tallest tree on the

farm. Raheem wrote this down.

'Okay everybody, let's find the compost bins NICE AND QUIETLY,' said Mira, taking charge.

They trotted round the back of the pigicorn pens. The pigicorns were asleep, surrounded by old bits of food and lots of mud. Dave farted approvingly.

Prrrrrrrrrr.

Mira gasped. 'It's a purr!' she whispered.

'Isn't it a pig fart?' whispered Darcy.

PRRRRRRRR.

The sound was coming from behind the compost bin. Mira slid off Dave and tiptoed to the compost bin. Dave was close behind her. She was so excited that she took a deep breath, then regretted it because of the smell. She squeezed her eyes shut to calm down, then peeped round the bin.

There they were! A grown-up caticorn had made a nest in the long grass and was snoozing. Beside her was a litter of four rainbow-coloured kitticorns and . . . Mira could hardly believe her eyes. ONE golden kitticorn!

'Awwww!' said Jake quietly.

'They actually *are* a bit cute in real life,' whispered Darcy.

Mira squealed in amazement. They were even more adorable than she had ever imagined. Her dream had come true!

Her squeal woke up the mother caticorn. She hissed loudly at Mira.

Mira turned to the group. 'See, they do hiss!' she said happily. Then she turned back to the nest. 'It's okay, lovely kitty,' she began. 'I'm your best friend –'

HIISSSSSSSSSSS! The caticorn stood up, arched her back and narrowed her eyes at Mira.

'Um, Mira, that doesn't sound like a happy

sound . . .' said Darcy.

Mira thought that *might* be true, but she couldn't help it. She just HAD to cuddle one! Carefully, she reached out a hand to stroke the golden kitticorn.

'Are you sure that's a good idea?' asked Raheem, who was standing *way* back by the compost bin.

Just as Mira's fingers were about to touch the golden kitticorn's fur, the mother caticorn gave an extra loud *HIISSSSSSSSSSSS*, waking up the rest of the kitticorns before she darted off behind the compost bin. The kitticorns scattered.

Mira's shoulders slumped. 'Why don't the kitticorns like me?' she asked. Dave shrugged and gave Mira a nuzzle.

Mira suddenly heard Darcy giggling. She turned around to see that her friend was *covered* in kitticorns. One was perched on Darcy's shoulders, another was sitting on her welly, and one kitticorn was curled up purring on her lap.

'Stop it, you guys, that tickles!' Darcy giggled, trying to stop one of the kitticorns licking her ear.

Dave chose that moment to do a massive poo right next to Darcy, which spooked the kitticorns and made them run off.

'Phew, thanks, Dave,' said Darcy, brushing pastel-coloured fur off her jumper. 'That was a bit much.'

'Why do they like you and not me?' asked Mira. She took out her portable poo shovel and miserably cleaned up Dave's poo.

'What can I say?' asked Darcy, with a flick of her hair. 'I have a magnetic personality.'

Even Jake was cuddling a kitticorn now. Mira had never seen him so happy! The kitticorn cuteness had got to him, too. Mira felt really left out.

Raheem checked his watch. 'We should return the chickicorn and get back to the bus. Let's get these kitticorns back to the nest.'

Mira hung back while the others rounded up the kittens and put them safely back into the caticorn's nest. The mother soon settled down happily next to them.

'Let's head back to the chickicorn barn!' said Jake, still grinning from his kitticorn cuddle.

Mira took one last, sad look at the nest. The four little rainbow kitticorns were settling down in a sleepy way. But the mother caticorn was looking around in a worried way . . .

'Wait!' said Mira.

'You've already tried to make them like you,' said Darcy impatiently. 'You've just got to let it go.'

'No,' said Mira. 'The golden kitticorn isn't in

the nest!'

The mother caticorn was pacing around now and meowing loudly, calling for her missing baby. Mira swallowed guiltily. She'd been so focused on trying to cuddle the kitticorns that she'd forgotten Bruce said that caticorns were easily scared. She hadn't been very careful at all!

They looked everywhere around the bins and the pigicorn pens, for any tiny little space the kitticorn could have run into. The mother caticorn's meows were getting louder and more worried. They strained their ears, but they couldn't hear the kitticorn anywhere.

What they did hear was a loud scratching sound. Dave was by the Doglark tree, scratching

his bum on the trunk.

'Oh, Dave, you could at least help!' said Mira crossly.

Dave stopped. And then he ran backwards at Mira and swooshed his tail in her face.

'PAH!' said Mira, trying to push Dave's tail away. 'Stop it!'

Then Dave ducked his head and started running in and out of Mira's ankles. The two of them got tangled up and fell to the ground.

'What are you doing, Dave?' said Mira helplessly. 'We've got to find the kitticorn – we don't have time for mucking around!'

Dave sighed, then dropped to the ground on his back. He waggled his hooves in the air, and then pointed straight upwards.

Mira looked up.

There, on the tallest branch of the tallest tree on the farm, was the golden kitticorn.

CHAPTER SEVEN
Rescue Mission

'Great,' said Darcy. 'So now we've stolen a chickicorn AND got a kitticorn stuck up a tree.'

'AND we could miss the bus home!' said Jake crossly.

Mira felt a tear roll down her cheek. She'd been so excited to come to BARCC and meet all the animals and learn about the farm and make best friends with a kitticorn. And win an awesome quest medal. But it had all gone wrong. She sniffed and wiped her nose on her sleeve.

Raheem, Darcy and Jake were all calling up

to the kitticorn. Jake was even making mewing sounds. But the golden kitticorn was very high up in the tree, and didn't seem like it was going to move any time soon.

Mira looked for Dave. She wanted to say sorry for not realising that he'd been trying to tell her where the kitticorn was. But she couldn't see Dave anywhere!

She realised then that she hadn't really been paying Dave much attention on this trip at all. All she had thought about were kitticorns. Dave must know she didn't love kitticorns more than him, she thought. He was her UBFF! But then she remembered Dave's sad expression at the picnic. Maybe he DID think she loved kitticorns more – and maybe that was why he'd gone!

Mira started looking frantically around. The others were helping the kitticorn. *She* needed to find Dave.

'Here kitty, kitty, kitty!' called Darcy. 'Come on down! We promise Mira won't try to stroke you again!'

'Dave!' Mira called. 'Dave, where are you? I'm sorry, Dave, come back!'

Just as Mira started to panic, she heard the sound of hooves thudding through the sparklecorn behind her. She turned around and saw Dave running as fast as his little legs could carry him. He had Mira's lunchbox in his mouth.

'You came back!' Mira gave her unicorn a huge hug. Dave was out of breath from running so fast.

'I didn't notice he was gone,' asked Jake. 'More importantly, how are we going to get this kitticorn down from this massive tree?'

Dave dropped the lunchbox on the ground. A packet of custard creams fell out.

'I thought you ate them all – oh! Dave! You're actually a genius!' Mira gasped. She gave him another hug and the little unicorn blushed.

'I don't get what's happening,' said Jake. 'Why is Dave a genius?'

Mira grinned widely. 'Kitticorns love custard creams! Quick, let's see if we can persuade this little one to come down.'

Mira took a custard cream out of the packet and held it out for the golden kitticorn to see. Sure enough, the kitticorn crept to the edge of a branch and then climbed down a couple of branches.

'Yay! Keep going!' Darcy started clapping.

The kitticorn kept jumping down. Then it suddenly slipped. Mira's heart was in her mouth as it dangled from a high branch, mewing pitifully.

'We have to help it!' Jake cried. He jumped up but couldn't reach the branch. He stood on Pegasus's back and tried to reach again.

'It's still too high for you,' said Darcy.

'Yes, thanks, that's really helpful,' Jake muttered with a frown. 'Come on, Mira. I need your help. Climb up on my shoulders.'

Mira hung back. 'But it doesn't like me! Can't someone else do it?'

'I'm too scared,' said Raheem.

'And I'm taking a picture. Smile!' Darcy held up her phone for a group pic.

Mira took a deep breath. She knew she had to help the kitticorn. After all, if she hadn't disturbed the nest the kitticorn wouldn't be stuck up the tree in the first place!

Dave nuzzled her arm and gave an encouraging fart. It was just what Mira needed.

'Thanks Dave,' she said gratefully.

With the packet of custard creams between her teeth, Mira started to clamber up on to Pegasus's back. Dave gave her a helpful shove with his muzzle. Carefully, she climbed on to Jake's shoulders. Wobbling slightly, she stretched out her arm. She *still* couldn't reach the kitticorn.

'I think we need Dave!' she called down.

'Does it have to be Dave?' said Jake, but Mira's plump little UBFF was already climbing on to Pegasus, doing little farts with the effort. Pegasus looked pained.

Dave eventually climbed on to Mira's
shoulders. She passed him the custard creams
and he reached up his hoof. The kitticorn hung
upside down, looking at Dave and blinking. Mira
could see that it was so scared it didn't know
what to do.

'Come on!' Mira pleaded.

Dave farted one more time.

Startled, the kitticorn let go of the branch,
fell on to Dave's nose and wrapped its tiny paws
around Dave's horn. The chickicorn popped
its head out of Dave's mane and cheeped. The
kitticorn squeaked and jumped, sliding off Dave
and down into Mira's arms.

The kitticorn was so surprised that it lay

completely still in Mira's arms for a moment. Its fur was super-soft and its little heart was beating quickly. It smelled of warm grass and custard creams. Despite being balanced on Jake's shoulders and a long way from the ground, Mira

felt a moment of total bliss.

Then the kitticorn ran down her legs and off Jake's back. With one big leap from Pegasus's bottom, it scampered away behind the pigicorn pens and back into its nest.

Dave and Mira climbed down more carefully.

Darcy and Raheem gave them all a round of applause. Mira high-fived her friends and pulled Dave close for a huge hug.

'You're the best, Dave,' she whispered in her unicorn's fluffy ear. 'Come on Team Awesome, let's get that chickicorn back and go home.'

MEEOW!

Mira turned to see the entire caticorn family standing in a line, staring at her. Before she could say 'uh-oh', the adorable kitticorns ran in and out of her ankles, purring. Then they all dropped to the ground and flailed their legs in the air, allowing her to tickle their tummies, before disappearing back behind the bins.

'Are you about to cry again?' asked Darcy.

There was a big lump in Mira's throat as she smiled. 'My books says when they do that, it means they REALLY like you!' she said.

'Honestly?' said Darcy. 'More than when they give you loads of cuddles and kisses like they did for me and Jake?'

Raheem coughed. 'Let's just get to the chickicorn barn, shall we?'

∪∪∪

Mira thought Dave would be a bit tired after all the excitement, so she gave him some more custard creams for energy (after leaving some by the compost bin for the caticorn family to enjoy later).

When they reached the chickicorn hatching

barn, Mira slid the barn door open. All the
chickicorns were sitting happily in their nests and
cheeping. Mira picked up the chickicorn from
Dave's mane and dropped it carefully into one
of the rainbow-straw hatching nests.

'There you go!' she said brightly. 'Just like Dave's mane. But better!'

The chickicorn looked up at her. Quick as a flash it jumped out of the straw and hopped back up on to Dave's head.

CHEEP!

Mira tried again and again and again, but each time the chickicorn jumped back on to Dave and burrowed into his mane.

Then Mira got Dave to stand outside the barn. She picked up the chick, ran into the barn, put it down, raced back out as fast as she could, slid the barn door shut and returned to Dave. He hung his head and snuffled.

Mira gave his ears a tickle. 'Aww, I know you

liked that chick, Dave. But don't worry, it will always be right here.' Mira pointed to his heart.

'No, it won't,' said Darcy.

'Sshh!' said Mira. 'I'm trying to make Dave feel better!'

'Yes, but the chickicorn is back.'

Darcy pointed. Sure enough, there was the little fluffy blue chick, perhed on top of Dave's big round bottom.

'Argh! We've got to get back!' cried Mira. 'What are we going to do? THIS is your home, little chickicorn!'

Darcy was inspecting her nails. 'The trouble is that the chickicorn thinks Dave *is* home,' she explained. 'The chick jumped on him as soon as it hatched. It thinks that Dave is its mum.'

'That's it!' cried Mira. 'Darcy, you're a genius!'

'Well, duh,' said Darcy, fluffing her hair. 'Why this time in particular?'

Mira raced back into the barn. 'There you are!' she said, scooping up a sad-looking, light-blue henicorn with a bent horn. 'There's someone you need to meet.'

Cluck cluck cluck.

The chickicorn popped its head up from Dave's tail. *Cheep?*

Cluck!

Cheep! CHEEP!

The henicorn hopped out of Mira's arms just as the chickicorn slid down Dave's tail.

They ran towards each other in a flurry of *clucks* and *cheeps*.

The chickicorn had found its *real* mum!

CHAPTER EIGHT
Gift-tastic

Mira really was proud of Dave. She knew it was always hard saying goodbye to your friends. She hated saying goodbye to Dave when she left Unicorn School, but at least she knew she was always coming back soon. She gave her UBFF an extra big pat as they all raced back through the sparklecorn field.

Riding beside Mira, Raheem looked glum.

'Are you okay?' Mira asked.

Raheem shrugged. 'I just would have liked to finish the quest.'

'We still had three more answers to find. It was really hard,' Mira consoled her friend.

'Actually we found two more,' said Raheem. '"What hisses but is not a snake" was kitticorns, and "what has a bark but no bite" was the Doglark tree.'

'Whoa!' said Darcy. 'We finished the quest and

you didn't say anything?'

'Raheem, that's awesome!' said Jake.

Raheem shook his head. 'No,' he said. 'We still have the last riddle to solve.'

Jake stopped suddenly. 'Where is everyone?'

'We've missed the bus!' Raheem started to panic.

'Chill, they're in the – ARGH!' Darcy pulled Star up so quickly that the others bumped into her.

Mira started panicking now. 'What's wrong? Have they gone without us?'

'No,' said Darcy. 'Nobody told me there was a gift shop! There's no time to waste!'

They all galloped towards the shop in the

visitor centre, where they could see the rest of
Class Red choosing pencils and rubbers and
cuddly horned toys. Mira breathed a sigh of relief
as they joined their classmates. They'd returned
the chickicorn, met lots of kitticorns *and* hadn't
missed the bus home. Phew!

Miss Glitterhorn was upstairs in the café,
surrounded by empty teacups and reading a book.
She looked happier than she had in ages.

Seb and his unicorn, Firework, were trying
out all the rainbow-coloured art pencils. Jake
and Pegasus bought matching skull-and-
crossbone rainbow badges. Darcy and Star
trotted past wearing feather boas and unicorn-
horn headbands, heading for the lift to the café.

Raheem was showing Brave the books about animal facts. And Flo was squealing with delight at all the cuddly toys.

Mira left Dave at the café having a large hot chocolate (with extra marshmallows) and headed downstairs again to join Flo.

'Mira, I can't decide which kitticorn to get! Do you like the pink one or the lavender one?' Flo was holding up two kitticorn cuddly toys. 'OR should I get this life-size lambicorn OR this slothicorn? I just can't decide!'

Mira laughed. 'They're all super cool.' She reached into a basket of toy chickicorns and rummaged around until she found a pale blue one. She smiled. She knew Dave would love it.

Bruce Hasselhoof appeared at the gift-shop doorway. He looked different. His eyes were a bit wild and his hair was standing up all over the place. Mira wondered if Class Red were more energetic than their usual visitors.

'Who did it?' Bruce cried.

'Who did what?' asked Freya.

'The field . . . my . . . sparklecorn, it's . . . it's all . . . hoof-marks . . . flattened!'

'Bruce, you're not making any sense,' said Freya.

Miss Glitterhorn stormed down the stairs from the café. 'Who on EARTH flattened the sparklecorn field?' she shouted. 'Class Red, this is unacceptable.'

Miss Glitterhorn did *not* look relaxed any more. Mira gulped. They'd only flattened one square metre, she thought. Although they had trotted back and forth through the sparklecorn several times . . .

'Hey! We made a maze!' Darcy yelled from upstairs.

Everyone looked up at Darcy on the café balcony. She waved at them to join her. Bruce Hasselhoof took the stairs two at a time. Class Red followed a little more slowly. Miss Glitterhorn looked at the lift, but it was full of unicorns, so she climbed the stairs too. Soon everyone was on the café balcony, looking out at the flattened sparklecorn field.

Mira's throat felt dry. They had flattened a LOT more corn than she realised.

Bruce cleared his throat. 'This is unbelievable.'

Miss Glitterhorn put her hands on her hips. 'Darcy, Mira, Raheem and Jake. What *have*

you been doing? Have you damaged BARCC
property? If I find that you ran away from Bruce's
carefully planned awesome activities, then there
will be consequences! As Bruce said, that sort of
behaviour is totally unacceptable!'

'No, no,' said Bruce faintly. 'I said it was
un*believable*. Not unacceptable. There was a maze
here back when I completed the quest, but it got
overgrown. I've wanted another one ever since.'

'So for a million years,' said Darcy.

Bruce ignored Darcy. 'Mazes are *amazing*!' he
said in delight.

Miss Glitterhorn didn't know what to say, so
Darcy quickly started three cheers for the new
maze before she could tell them off.

Raheem rummaged in his backpack.

He pulled out the quest checklist and

cleared his throat.

'Um, Mr Hasselhoof? I think we've sort of completed the quest.'

The rest of Class Red gasped. Bruce and Miss Glitterhorn hurried over and looked at their checklist. Raheem explained how they'd found the answers to the first four riddles.

'And then, number five is "An amazing sight inside which you cannot see",' he continued. 'Well, you just said that our maze in the sparklecorn field is "amazing" and we couldn't see it when we were inside it.'

'Wonderful work!' Bruce was ecstatic. 'That question must be left over from when we had the old maze. No wonder no one ever completed the quest. But you DID!' His face fell. 'Oh, but there are no quest medals. No one's completed it for so long that we just stopped keeping them in stock.'

Darcy gave Mira a nudge. 'I'm sorry, Mira. I know you love medals.'

Mira hugged her friend. 'You know what?' she said. 'Today was so awesome it doesn't need a medal.'

'NO, WAIT!' Bruce dashed off. He came back a minute later holding a welly from the welly station with 'BARCC Medal' written on it in mud. 'You can take this as a trophy of your excellence.'

Jake snatched it off Bruce before anyone else could get their hands on it. 'As unofficial quest leader, I think I deserve to keep this,' he said.

Dave trotted up and nibbled the toe off the welly so now it said, 'BARCC Me'.

137

Mira, Raheem and Darcy burst into laughter. They high-fived Jake and he joined in with the laughter too.

Bruce clapped his hands. 'Right-o, kids, time to get rid of you! Ha ha, only joking. But seriously, get on the bus.'

Class Red scrambled to buy their souvenirs and then lined up outside the bus. Miss Glitterhorn was collecting clipboards and ticking the children's names off her list as they got on board.

'Raheem, Seb, Freya, Flo – hang on, Flo, what's that on your back?' Miss Glitterhorn said, stopping Flo.

'What's what?' said Flo, turning around in circles to look behind her. Mira saw that Flo was wearing a cute furry slothicorn backpack.

'I didn't see any of those backpacks for sale in the shop. Where were they? Can I go back and get one?' demanded Darcy.

Bruce Hasselhoof let out a yelp. 'That's not a backpack, it's a real slothicorn! What did I say the first rule of BARCC was, guys?'

'Stay where I can see you at all times,' said Raheem.

'Ah. But the MOST important rule is DO NOT take the baby animals home!' said Bruce.

'Oopsie!' said Flo. 'I didn't realise we were still cuddling. He must have fallen asleep on me. Here you go.'

She carefully peeled the slothicorn off her back

and handed him to Bruce. The slothicorn
stirred but quickly fell asleep again and started
snoring on Bruce's shoulder.

∪∪∪

As the Rainbow Bus pulled away from BARCC and started making its way back to Unicorn School, Mira went to sit next to Jake.

'Thanks for all your help today, Jake,' she said.

Jake grinned. 'I guess it *was* kind of cool meeting the kitticorns.'

Mira reached into her gift-shop bag and pulled out a small cuddly toy kitticorn. She handed it to Jake. 'Sorry they didn't have a golden one.'

Jake's eyes got really wide. 'Is that really for me?'

Mira nodded. Jake took the kitticorn toy from her tentatively.

'No one's ever given me a present at Unicorn School before,' he said.

Mira smiled as Jake cradled the toy in his arms.

'I mean, obviously I get presents all the time at home,' he added quickly.

'Okay,' said Mira.

Then Jake leaned into Pegasus and fell asleep.

Dave was snoring softly next to Mira. She pulled the blue chickicorn toy out of her bag and tucked it into Dave's mane, so it would always remind him of the cute and cuddly chickicorn that he'd looked after so well.

Then Mira looked around the bus at all her classmates dozing, snuggled up to their unicorns. They'd learned a lot at BARCC. They'd learned about the importance of soil and sparklecorn. They'd learned that goaticorns eat, well, everything, and how not to take a slothicorn home with you. But they'd also learned that shiny medals weren't the be-all and end-all. What really mattered was having an awesome time with your friends and taking care of each other. With the added bonus of being able to brag to Rani when she got home about winning a quest!

All Mira had wanted this morning was a kitticorn cuddle. But the most important thing she'd learned today was something she'd always known, deep down. That cuddles from her UBFF were the very best of all.

Mira snuggled into Dave, who gave a sleepy fart. And a moment later she was fast asleep, too.

WHICH ANIMAL-ICORN ARE YOU?

1. *Would you rather have a cosy film night at home or go out to the cinema?*
   a. Movies at home please! My sofa is so comfy. I'll make the popcorn.
   b. I would rather sleep.
   c. Let's go out! The cinema is so exciting.
   d. I don't mind as long as there are snacks. Did you say doughnuts?

2. *Would you rather live in a forest or a shed?*
   a. A nice, warm shed, please. With lots of rainbow straw.
   b. I don't mind, I can sleep anywhere.
   c. Ooh the forest would be awesome!
   d. The shed, as long as there are snacks there.

3. *At school, would you rather be amazing at music or science?*
   a. Music – to accompany my friends in a singalong.
   b. Music sends me to sleeeeeeeep.
   c. Science is super cool.
   d. Science so I could invent new snacks.

4. *Would you rather play football or chess?*
   a. Chess – I like indoor games.
   b. I'm too sleepy for games.

c. Football! Let's go!
d. Is it chocolate football or chocolate chess?

5. *For your birthday, would you rather have a crafts or trampolining party?*
   a. Crafts – I like making woolly pompoms.
   b. Zzzzzzzzz.
   c. Trampolining – woohoo!
   d. Just the cake for me, thanks.

6. *If you were a superhero, would you rather be invisible or be able to fly?*
   a. Invisible. Chickens can't fly.
   b. Invissizzzzzzz.
   c. Fly! That would be awesome!
   d. I would like to be invisible and be able to fly to find the best snacks.

Answers

Mostly As: you're a chickicorn! Sweet and fluffy, you know there's no place like home!

Mostly Bs: you're a slothicorn! You're – yawn – just – yawn – soooo sleepy zzzzz.

Mostly Cs: you're a kitticorn! Cute and playful, you're always full of energy.

Mostly Ds: you're Dave the unicorn! You love snacks and getting your own way, but you're always there for your friends.

UNICORN JOKES

What do you call a cold unicorn?
A blue-nicorn

What do you call a scary unicorn?
A boo-nicorn

What do you call a unicorn with a toffee stuck in its teeth?
A chew-nicorn

What do you call a unicorn trying to solve a mystery?
A clue-nicorn

What do you call a unicorn that's bigger in the mornings?
He grew-nicorn

What do you call an artistic unicorn?
A drew-nicorn

What do you call a lady sheep with a horn on her head?
A ewe-nicorn

What do you call a unicorn with the sniffles?
A flu-nicorn

What do you call a unicorn on safari?
A gnu-nicorn

What do you call a unicorn crossing its legs?
A need-the-loo-nicorn

What do you call a relieved unicorn?
A phew!-nicorn

Catch up on all of Mira and Dave's adventures at Unicorn School!

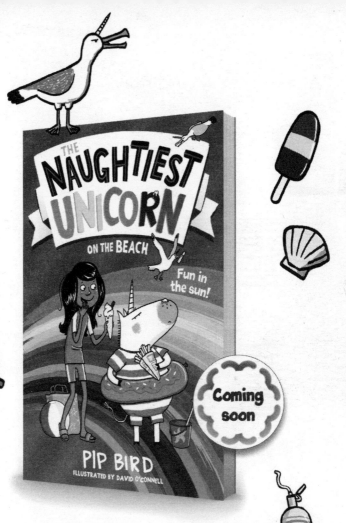

THE NAUGHTIEST UNICORN ON THE BEACH

Fun in the sun!

Coming soon

PIP BIRD

ILLUSTRATED BY DAVID O'CONNELL

Time for fun in the sun at UNICORN SCHOOL!

EGMONT